WARRIOR HEROES

THE KNIGHT'S ENEMIES

First published 2014 by A & C Black
An imprint of Bloomsbury Publishing Plc
50 Bedford Square, London WC1B 3DP

www.bloomsbury.com

Bloomsbury is a registered trademark of Bloomsbury Publishing Plc

ISBN 978-1-4729-0439-3

A CIP catalogue for this book is available from the British Library.

Printed and bound by CPI Group (UK) Ltd, Croydon CR0 4YY

1 3 5 7 9 10 8 6 4 2

WARRIOR HEROES

THE KNIGHT'S ENEMIES

BENJAMIN HULME-CROSS

Illustrated by
Angelo Rinaldi

A & C BLACK
AN IMPRINT OF BLOOMSBURY
LONDON NEW DELHI NEW YORK SYDNEY

CONTENTS

INTRODUCTION
THE HALL OF HEROES

The Hall of Heroes is a museum
all about warriors throughout
history. It's full of swords, bows
and arrows, helmets, boats, armour,
shields, spears, axes and just
about anything else that a warrior
might need. But this isn't just
another museum full of old stuff
in glass cases - it's also haunted
by the ghosts of the warriors whose
belongings are there.

Our great grandfather, Professor
Blade, set up the museum and when
he died he started haunting the
place too. He felt guilty about the
trapped ghost warriors and vowed he
would not rest in peace until all
the other ghosts were laid to rest
first. And that's where Arthur and
I come in…

On the night of the Professor's
funeral Arthur and I broke into the
museum – we knew it was wrong but
we just couldn't help ourselves. And
that's when we discovered something
very weird. When we are touched by
one of the ghost warriors we get
transported to the time and place
where the ghost lived and died.
And we can't get back until we've
fixed whatever it is that keeps the
ghost from resting in peace. So we
go from one mission to the next,
recovering lost swords, avenging
deaths, saving loved ones or doing
whatever else the ghost warrior
needs us to do.

Fortunately while the Professor
was alive I wrote down everything
he ever told us about these

warriors in a book I call *Warrior Heroes* - so we do have some idea of what we're getting into each time - even if Arthur does still call me 'Finn the geek'. But we need more than a book to survive each adventure because wherever we go we're surrounded by war and battle and the fiercest fighters who ever lived, as you're about to find out!

CHAPTER 1

The Professor ushered the boys into his office with a hushed command, "Hurry boys, it won't be long until he arrives." He had just announced that the next warrior to ask for their help would be a medieval knight.

"A quest!" Arthur's eyes gleamed as the door closed behind them. "Now that sounds like a *real* adventure!"

Finn snorted. "Quest! You can forget all that King Arthur stuff."

Arthur rolled his eyes at his brother's attitude.

The Professor nodded. "Finn's right. They didn't really go in for quests in the way that the stories suggest."

The boys were in their great grandfather's study at the museum sitting around his desk. A single desk lamp cast very little light around the rest of the room.

Finn leaned forward. "Who is this knight then?" he asked. A clock sitting on the mantle piece ticked and whirred.

"I'm afraid we don't really know much about him old boy," the Professor replied. "He lived in England. We think it was during the twelfth or thirteenth centuries but that's about all the information we have so we'll just have to ask him when he gets here. He'll be along soon enough."

"Well what did knights get up to then?" Arthur enquired. "Jousting? Rescuing damsels? Fighting for the king?"

"Fighting against the king more like," said Finn. Arthur scowled as his brother corrected him again. "There were civil wars and rebellions. Every time a king died a whole bunch of people would claim the right to be the next king and whoever won the argument then spent the rest of his or her life trying to fight off challengers."

The Professor smiled. "He's right again Arthur. Jousting tournaments did happen but the knights' main job was to fight for their lord whenever he needed them. They didn't really fight for the king as such unless that is what their lord told them to do."

"Fine, whatever," Arthur snapped. "I wonder if we'll get to wear armour and ride horses."

"I hate to disappoint you," said the Professor as Arthur sighed and began tapping an impatient foot, "Most knights would have worn chain mail at that time rather than armour plates. And a lot of the fighting revolved around castles – laying siege to them or defending them. You didn't need horses so much for that, although you did need a horse to be a knight."

"So they were basically soldiers then?"

"Exactly," the Professor agreed. "They were well-trained soldiers who could fight on horseback in battle or alongside peasants in castle sieges. They were officers in small armies –"

"Shh!" Finn broke in. "I think I heard something."

They listened intently. The clock had stopped ticking, and the only sound to break the silence was a steady clink as somebody approached the door of the study.

The air in the room grew colder. The lamp fizzed and cut out, plunging the room into darkness. Arthur and Finn were used to the routine but still their muscles tingled with anticipation. The door creaked open and closed.

Nobody dared move for a minute. Then, carefully, the Professor lit a candle and its thin, flickering light faintly illuminated the figure of a knight. His scarred face was smeared with blood that seeped down from under his chain mail hood and the expression he wore as he cast his stare around the room was one of pure anguish.

The boys both stood frozen to the spot, hardly daring to breathe. The Professor cleared his throat. "How can my boys help you old chap?"

The knight's gaze shifted slowly from one boy to the other. "Eleanor..." he moaned, the word coming out like a sigh.

"Who was..." Finn faltered. "Who is she?"

"Eleanor," the bloodied knight sighed again. His head slumped forward and his shoulders heaved. "My daughter."

"My dear man," said the Professor, clearing his throat again. "What happened to her?"

"Wroxley Castle was under siege," the knight began. "It was John the Withered who attacked us. A cruel man. A very cruel man."

"And that is how you died?" The Professor asked. "What is your name?"

"Sir William Mallory," said the knight, looking at the Professor for the first time. "Yes, yes, I died in the siege at the hands of a traitor."

"And Eleanor?"

The knight groaned again. "They took her. A spy kidnapped her during the siege. My only child and her mother long since dead."

"Then she lived?" Arthur prompted.

The knight shook his head slightly in his chain mail hood.

"Instead of making the peasants fear him John wanted *the lords* to fear him instead."

Sir William broke off and put his hands to his head. "They sent Eleanor's head back to me the following morning..." he trailed off, seeming to gasp for air.

Finn stole a glance over at his brother, whose horrified expression mirrored his own. Cautiously, he said, "Then you want us to –"

"Save her!" Sir William cried. "Save her! Save her in any way you can!" Sir William lurched forward towards the boys, hands outstretched.

"Wait! You need to tell us more!" Arthur shouted but it was too late. A ghostly hand gripped each boy by the neck. The air filled with mist so thick that nothing of the room could be seen, the candle flickered and died and the boys saw only darkness.

CHAPTER 2

Arthur became aware of a steady far-away roar, like that of the sea heard from a distance. His mind reached out towards the sound and it grew louder but though he blinked his eyes against the darkness, he could still see nothing. Gradually he began to make out more sounds intermingled with the roar. They were shouts, he realised, though they still sounded distant.

Where am I? He wondered, noticing for the first time how cold he was. The air around him began to move and he had the strange sensation that he was falling backwards.

Shadowy figures in front of a shimmering light appeared in front of him. It was only as his mouth filled with icy water that he realised he was looking up at the sky. *I'm underwater,* he thought calmly. And then he was awake. Terrified, he thrashed around in the water. His foot struck something hard and he kicked up towards daylight.

Chest burning, he shot up through the water and gulped in a huge, spluttering lungful of air as he broke the surface. He twisted around to the sound of shouting and saw that he was in a fast-flowing river. A steep, rocky bank was slipping quickly by in a blur of green.

"Quick boy!" someone yelled.

The water spun Arthur around as it whisked him along and he saw to his horror that he was fast approaching a water mill. Its giant paddles churned slowly through water that swirled and bubbled ominously.

He kicked and thrashed towards the bank and his hand brushed against a stone. It was worn smooth by the river and he slid inexorably on.

"Help!" he cried, swallowing mouthfuls of icy water as the paddles churned closer and closer.

"Here boy! You only have one chance." A man was sprinting along the bank next to Arthur and was soon ahead of him – in between him and the mill. The man reached down and held a long staff over the water. Arthur bobbed towards the staff, twisting desperately to position himself and a moment later he had it in both hands. His head dipped below the water as the current tugged him round. One hand slipped off the staff and as he felt the other beginning to slide he heard the creak of the mill and closed his eyes.

I wonder whether Finn will do any better, he thought as the relentless current sucked him on. Then strong hands gripped him by the wrists and dragged him out of the water, scraping his chest painfully over stones before rolling him onto his back where he lay, coughing water out of his lungs and blinking up at his rescuer. A big man with curly brown hair and a thick beard stared back at him.

Arthur sat up, still coughing and spluttered, "Where am I?"

"Where are you? The water must have washed away your wits. You are outside Wroxley Castle." The man nodded his head away from the river. Arthur looked and saw that a large stone wall rose up from the top of the river bank.

"Oh yes," he said. "Wroxley. I remember. Er... Thank you sir."

"You may have the chance to repay me sooner than you think," the man replied. "Men loyal to John the Withered advance on the castle as we speak, laying waste to the villages. People from miles hence are fleeing to the castle gates and begging to be admitted. I am one of them. Perchance you can persuade the guards to let me in."

"I hate to disappoint you," said Arthur,

thinking quickly. "But they don't know me at the castle either."

The man's face fell and he began walking briskly away. Clearly he had no more use for Arthur.

"Wait!" Arthur shouted. "Do you have a name? I'll tell them you saved me."

"I am Adam," the man replied over his shoulder without stopping. "We must get to the gatehouse. Soon they will close the gates."

* * * * *

Finn felt as though he was rattling around in a barrel with a brick. His head was banging repeatedly against something hard and his body was being shaken and bumped from all directions. He opened his eyes to the weak grey light that seeped through a forest canopy overhead. Something pressed hard on his leg and he looked down to see a pig rolling onto his foot. *I must be in some sort of cart*, he thought.

He pulled his leg back and tried to stand up, slipping and staggering backwards until his legs hit a low barrier and he toppled sideways out of the cart. He cursed as he landed hard on a muddy path.

A thin line of ragged, wretched-looking people were making their hurried way along the forest track, many of them wailing and groaning. A couple of people glanced briefly at the strange boy who had appeared but nobody stopped or spoke to him as they rushed past. Finn dusted himself off where he sat and waited for the miserable procession to pass, trying to remember where he was. For a few minutes everything was a blank. It always took a while to remember the details after shifting in time. Gradually Finn's mind cleared and he remembered Sir William. *Save his daughter Eleanor, that's the mission. But what does she need saving from?* His thoughts were interrupted by the steady beat of a horse's hooves.

A teenage boy on horseback rounded a bend in the track and slowed his mount to a canter as he approached Finn through the trees.

"Quick boy," the rider shouted, reining the horse in. "John the Withered and his men are a mile hence and advancing. They have laid waste to everything in their path and they are showing mercy to none. To Wroxley Castle if you value your life!"

Finn got to his feet warily.

"Which way?" he asked.

"Which way?" the young man looked at Finn as if he were an idiot. "Come," he said, reaching down. "Climb up. I am Thomas Shipton, squire. Your name?"

"Finn Blade, traveller," he said, making to grab hold of the friendly outstretched hand. As he did so he noticed a movement in the forest behind Thomas.

"Look out!" he shouted. Instinctively, Thomas hunched down into the horse's mane as an arrow hissed between the two boys and thudded into a tree.

The squire threw a panicked glance over his shoulder before turning back to Finn, "Climb up," he said urgently, holding out a slightly shakier hand this time. Finn grabbed it and swung himself up onto the horse behind Thomas just in time to avoid a second arrow that flew past at head height. Thomas kicked the horse's sides to speed them away, but as he did so the horse screamed and reared up. Finn slid backwards and landed hard in the mud for the second time that day while Thomas shouted in alarm as his horse staggered sideways on its hind legs and then toppled heavily to the ground, an arrow protruding from its flank. Finn felt the ground shake as the horse landed, pinning Thomas to the ground by his foot.

The archers gave a triumphant shout and Finn looked up to see two men roaring and running forwards. He crawled behind the horse and lay next to Thomas, whose foot was trapped beneath the heavy weight of the animal. The bow he had

slung across his back waggled in the air as he tried to kick himself free. Finn grabbed it and wrestled it up over Thomas' head.

"Arrows," he said breathlessly. Thomas pushed himself up on one elbow, revealing a quiver that had been trapped beneath him. Finn slipped the strap of the quiver over Thomas' head and snatched out an arrow, notching it to the bowstring with fluent ease. If he had to fight then archery was his thing. Taking a deep breath he pushed himself up on one knee and took aim at one of the archers. They were ten seconds away now at most, sprinting towards him, and their eyes widened as they saw the danger they were in. Finn drew the string back, took aim at the bigger of the two men and released. The man collapsed to the floor, gurgling horribly as he clutched at the arrow lodged in his throat. His companion stopped abruptly to raise his bow and reach back for an arrow. Finn did the same and time seemed to slow, the two adversaries knowing that life and death depended on being the first to shoot. In almost perfect unison they notched arrows and took aim. *Too close to call*, thought Finn, and as he let his arrow fly he ducked his head back down behind the horse. He heard the arrow whistle through the air and then felt the horse shudder slightly. At the same time the archer gave a shout of pain.

Finn notched a third arrow and sprang sideways out from behind the horse. He needn't have bothered. His enemy lay motionless on his back, an arrow buried deep in his chest.

Finn sank back to the ground, his heart

hammering. For a few moments there was complete silence. Then Thomas began calling out. "Finn? Are you hit? Finn?"

He crawled back around the horse to Thomas' side.

"Both dead," he panted.

"Then I owe you my life," said Thomas, wincing in pain. "But we must be gone else we will be killed before I can repay the debt." He tried again to pull his foot out from beneath the horse before slumping down and looking up at Finn desperately. Suddenly the horse whimpered and arched its back. The weight shifted and Thomas yanked his foot free. It was to be the horse's final act.

"Is she alive?" Thomas whispered. Finn looked at the motionless animal and saw that a second arrow was now lodged in her chest. He shook his head and Thomas' face grew pale.

"Come on," said Finn kindly. "I'll help you to the castle. Can you walk?"

"My ankle is bruised, that is all. I can walk."

Thomas and Finn set off along the track, glancing nervously over their shoulders from time to time. Finally they emerged from the forest and Finn caught his first sight of Wroxley Castle. He studied it hard, trying to take in and memorise every detail that could possibly be of use later.

The castle was simple but forbidding. Topped with battlements, the outer wall formed a square, each side of which looked to be around fifty metres long. The eastern side of the outer wall seemed to rise up out of a river which formed a natural defence against attack from that direction. A moat, fed by the river, bordered the other three sides of the wall. On the western side, away from the river, a large, square gatehouse thrust up and out from the outer wall, fortifying the entrance. Finn could not see clearly, but he knew from his conversations with the Professor that the drawbridge would provide access across the moat and through the gatehouse, which allowed defenders to protect the entrance.

The main castle building – the keep – was a huge, dark, cube of stone with four short towers jutting up from the top corners. It was strangely situated. Finn knew to expect the keep to sit in the centre of the space within the outer wall but this was not the case here. The castle stood right up against the eastern side of the outer wall by the river. In fact it looked as though the outer wall and the wall of the keep were one and the same at that point.

"A ready-made moat then," Finn observed.

"On one side at least," said Thomas. "They dug the moat around the other three sides."

They continued in silence for a while and they were quite close to the castle by the time Thomas stopped abruptly, frowning.

"That is strange," he said. "The drawbridge is up."

EXTRACT FROM *WARRIOR HEROES*
BY FINN BLADE

DEFENDING A CASTLE

Castles are built to be easy to
defend and very difficult to attack.
The first line of defence is usually
the castle moat — a huge, deep ditch
surrounding the whole castle, filled
either with water or sharp wooden
pikes. To get across the moat the
attackers need to find a way of laying
bridges across it, and while they do
this archers can pick attackers off
from the castle wall. Moats also make
it difficult for attacking armies
to dig tunnels under the castle to
'undermine' it.

The next line of defence is the

castle's outer wall and gatehouse. The whole of this outer wall is usually topped with battlements so that archers have huge stone blocks protecting them but can shoot through the gaps at the poorly protected attackers. Should enemy soldiers get as far as the outer wall and try to climb it, archers can rain arrows down on them from overhead, and if that isn't effective enough they sometimes pour boiling water over enemy heads.

Finally if somehow the enemy does get through or across the outer wall everyone can retreat back to the main castle building — the keep — which is the strongest structure in the whole complex and almost impossible to break into.

CHAPTER 3

Arthur stood at the back of a desperate mob who were shouting across the moat to the soldiers in the castle. *Where is Finn?* He thought, scanning the fields around the castle for any sign of his brother. *If he doesn't get here soon we'll have no chance!* He breathed a huge sigh of relief when he caught sight of Finn approaching and rushed over to meet him.

"Glad you could make it," he said to Finn. "They won't let anyone else in and they've pulled the drawbridge up."

Thomas frowned. "That is not Sir William's way," he said. "He is a kind lord. And if they are not admitted to the castle all these people will die."

"This is Thomas Shipton," Finn explained. "We helped each other out of some trouble earlier. Thomas, this is my older brother, Arthur."

"Your brother did all the helping, friend," said Thomas ruefully. "He saved my life. It appears I may be able to return the favour sooner than I had thought - they will not keep me out of the castle." With that he began to make his way through the crowd of people, Arthur and Finn following behind.

They reached the edge of the moat and Thomas turned to the furious group of men and women who were hurling a mixture of curses, insults and plaintive pleadings up at the guards on the castle walls and on top of the large gatehouse that surrounded the castle entrance. A tall, blonde-haired young man appeared and stared down at the group with a sneer. The group instantly fell quiet.

"Keep running!" he shouted down to the crowd. "If you stay here any longer you will be killed by John's men. That's if I don't give the order to kill you first!"

Thomas' face darkened. "Ralph," he spat.

"Not a friend of yours then?" Finn asked.

"An arrogant bully. And he is trying to court the woman I love."

"Where is Sir William?" someone called and the shouting began again.

"Friends!" Thomas shouted above the din. "Friends, quiet. Let me speak with the guards. They know me."

Ralph caught sight of Thomas and his sneer broadened into a malevolent grin.

"The castle is ready Thomas," he shouted. "We prepare to defend against John the Withered. Have you heard? We will – " a shout from somewhere beyond the wall caused him to stop abruptly and he turned away.

Moments later he turned back, his face scarlet. "Sir William instructs me to open the gates," he called out stiffly, "You may enter."

The crowd jeered and jostled as the drawbridge began a creaking descent over the moat. As soon as it reached the ground they stampeded over it and through the gatehouse with Thomas, Finn and Arthur bringing up the rear. The boys crossed the threshold of Wroxley Castle and stared up at its dark, looming walls as the gates thudded shut behind them.

"This feels like a prison compound," Arthur whispered.

"Yeah," Finn agreed. "This kind of courtyard inside the outer wall is called a bailey but prison compound is about right."

The new arrivals joined a throng of nervous-looking people in the compound, whispering to one another and glancing furtively up at the outer wall. Soldiers stared back at them from the top of the wall on either side of the gatehouse. Arthur spotted Adam talking intently to a woman through the crowd of people. He was about to go over and introduce Finn to the man who had rescued him earlier when someone called down to them.

"Friends!" the voice boomed. Finn and Arthur recognised the voice as quickly as they recognised the man. Sir William stood at the top of the outer wall and addressed the group.

"Every one of you is welcome to take refuge here. As you all know the army of John the Withered marches upon us. By nightfall we will be under siege. We have had very little time to prepare our defences and this afternoon we will need to accomplish much if we are to withstand the attack. I ask that each healthy man, woman and child make themselves available to assist in the defence of this castle in any way that they are asked to. Those of you who were able to bring food or livestock, please hand it over to my men to be added to our supplies. We do not know how long the siege may last and we may need every scrap of food we can lay our hands on." Sir William paused for a moment, his eyes sweeping the crowd.

"Now hear this. The punishment for any man or woman found stealing food is death. The punishment for any man or woman found to be spying for John the Withered is death. The punishment for any man or woman who attacks another within these walls is death. If we stand together we may prevail. If we falter we will be cut down and I need not tell you that John the Withered will not be merciful." There was complete silence.

"I must go now to finish our plans for the defence. For now, as best you can, take some rest. You will soon be called upon."

Sir William descended the stairs of the outer wall and strode through the crowd, who parted for him and called out their thanks as he disappeared into the castle.

Finn and Arthur looked at one another anxiously. "How are we ever going to get Eleanor out of this?" muttered Finn.

Thomas let out a sigh. "Eleanor," he murmured. The boys followed his gaze and saw that he was staring up at a blue ribbon fluttering out from a tiny slit of a window near the top of the keep.

"The woman you love?" Finn asked, trying to sound calm.

"That she is," said Thomas. "A fairer maiden

never walked this Earth. The ribbon at the window is for me."

Arthur grinned and pretended to vomit behind Thomas' back. "And she's in there is she?" he asked.

"Aye. Sir William will keep her there until the siege is over. It is the safest place for her. Though you may be sure she will challenge her father – she never cared much for safety..." Thomas trailed off, gazing wistfully up at the window. Without warning a tall, blonde man barged into him, sending him sprawling into the mud. He landed awkwardly and cried out as his wounded ankle hit the ground.

Ralph stood over him. "Poor Thomas, are you hurt?" he mocked. "My apologies, I did not see you in my haste. My lady Eleanor signals to me by that ribbon that she desires my company."

Thomas leapt to his feet and lurched towards Ralph with one hand on the hilt of his sword but Arthur grabbed his arm and held him back. "Remember what Sir William said about attacking anyone," Finn advised as Arthur tightened his grip on Thomas' arm.

Furious, Thomas struggled for a moment but finally he relented.

"The boy is right, Thomas. Listen to your new playmate." Ralph goaded in a child-like voice. "Now I must go. Eleanor awaits and Sir William will be requiring my presence at the battle council."

Arthur snorted. "He didn't care much for your decision about keeping this lot out, but yes I'm *sure* he needs your advice now."

Sir Ralph's eyes widened in shock. "How dare you. I'll have you flogged you insolent dog." He sprang forward and grabbed Arthur roughly by the throat. "What is your name?" he hissed.

Arthur struggled, coughing and choking – pulling at Ralph's hands in a desperate bid to free himself.

A circle had gathered around Arthur and Sir Ralph, formed entirely of the people who had just arrived at the castle.

"The boy's right," someone called out. "You tried to turn us away and Sir William showed us kindness. Leave the boy alone!"

Sir Ralph's face reddened again and he spun round to face this new tormenter, pulling Arthur with him. But before the situation could develop any further, a thick-set man stepped out of the crowd. It was Adam, Arthur realised.

"Sir William is waiting for you Sir," he said.

Sir Ralph, though furious, saw that this was his chance to leave before his embarrassment became any worse. Flashing a final, hard stare at Arthur, he released his grip and stalked away with Adam towards the castle.

Arthur fell, coughing to the ground. Finn and Thomas hurried over to him and helped him up before leading him to the outer wall. They all sat down and Thomas drew a deep breath.

"Now you too have saved my life Arthur. I would have tried to kill him. What in God's name possessed me? He is a knight and I a squire."

"I can think of a few other words to describe him," said Arthur, still struggling to draw breath. "You should not have said what you did. I thank you for it but Sir Ralph will not forget. He is a cruel man and he hates to be challenged. We must all watch each other's backs." Thomas rubbed his ankle. "By heaven this has been a day to remember already eh Finn? Both of us were nearly killed in the forest. I nearly attacked a knight moments after being warned that the penalty is death. And Arthur here has already made an enemy."

"Actually I nearly died earlier too," said Arthur and he filled them in on his near-drowning experience, omitting the part about waking up from time travel at the bottom of a river.

"Strange," Thomas mused. "So this Adam saved your life? I thought nothing of it at the time in my anger, but I have never seen him before and now he is running messages for Sir William."

Arthur shrugged. "There must be lots of people here today who you don't know. What's it like normally?"

Thomas explained to Finn and Arthur that he lived in Wroxley Castle as a squire to Sir William's brother, Sir Godfrey. Sir William's daughter Eleanor lived there also and she and

Thomas had fallen in love, though he could not openly court her until he was knighted. But then the cruel and malicious Ralph had arrived, knighted too young in Sir William's view. He had little choice but to take Ralph in though as he was the son of a wealthy Baron and the new arrival had made no secret of his admiration for Eleanor. In addition there was also a small troop of pages, squires, maids-in-waiting, castle guards and servants who lived in and around the castle.

"So when will you be knighted?" Finn asked.

"I know not," Thomas sighed. "I am only seventeen years. Too young for knighthood in any ordinary circumstances."

"And does Sir William know about you and Eleanor?" Arthur enquired, trying and failing to hide his smile.

"Faith no!" said Thomas. "And he must not!"

A young boy approached them from among the crowd of people and they all fell silent. "Master Thomas, Sir Godfrey summons you."

"Farewell my friends," said Thomas, getting to his feet, and hopping slightly on his bruised ankle. "I will find you this evening, and in the meantime remember, keep away from Sir Ralph. John the Withered is not the only man you should fear."

CHAPTER 4

Arthur and Finn had spent the day helping the soldiers to prepare the defences. Barrels of cold water, quivers full of arrows, large bows, spears, lances and various other weapons were now stacked neatly along the outer wall behind the battlements in readiness for the inevitable attack.

Guards stood along the top of the outer wall,

with even more backing them up from the top of the castle.

Arthur stood on the outer wall, leaning against the battlements and gazing out across the fields. The setting sun smeared heavy clouds with pink and purple, rendering the whole scene beautiful and strangely calm. Yet the situation was neither. Just beyond the range of the castle archers, an army had made their camp. All afternoon the soldiers and their supplies had trickled out of the forest and onto the plain, swarming like ants around the castle until they had it surrounded on three sides, with the river containing the fortress from the east. Tents and flags had been erected, fires lit and other more sinister preparations made.

Looking west Arthur could see a row of

huge wooden catapults lined up, ready for a full frontal assault on the gatehouse and outer wall. *Trebuchets, not catapults,* Finn would have reminded him.

An enormous tree had been felled and transported from the forest to sit behind the catapults where a small group of men were hammering away at it, presumably to fashion a battering ram.

To the north a group of men appeared to be constructing some sort of wooden tower on wheels.

"A siege engine," said Finn in a hushed tone, walking over to stand with Arthur. "They use them to wheel soldiers up to the castle wall so they don't have to climb. I can't believe this is happening. We're actually in a full on medieval castle siege. Nice helmet by the way."

Arthur put a hand up to straighten his oversized helmet. Both he and Finn had been given them in preparation for the battle. Arthur wasn't sure whether Finn sounded geekily excited or frightened. "Yeah," he said. "And we're going to be on the front line with the archers. Are you OK with that?" When Thomas had told the castle Sergeant about Finn's prowess with a bow and arrow the boys had swiftly been instructed to join the archers when the attack began.

"I'm trying not to think about it," said Finn. "But listen, how are we going to get to Eleanor? We've got to get inside the keep."

"And why is that?" came a deep voice. The two boys jumped in surprise and turned to see that Adam had appeared at their side.

"Oh!" Arthur smiled. "Hello Adam. Hey, thanks so much for calling Ralph away before. That's the second time you've helped me today – I really owe you now. Had Sir William really summoned him?"

Adam shook his head. "No, but I did what I could. You have a hot head my young friend. You should be careful around men like Sir Ralph."

"Well, thanks again. This is my brother Finn by the way. We were just wondering whether we could see inside the keep at some point."

Adam looked at Arthur strangely, but before he could speak one of the guards on top of the gatehouse blew a horn, signalling that someone was approaching the castle.

A single horse and rider were racing towards the castle from the direction of the trebuchets.

A knight who bore some resemblance to Sir William dashed out from the keep and mounted the steps of the outer wall two at a time. The rider reined in his horse and slowed to a stop on the other side of the moat.

"I bring a message from John the Withered!" the man shouted. "Where is Sir William?"

The knight appeared at the top of the gatehouse. "I am Sir Godfrey, Sir William's brother. What is your message?"

The rider smiled. "John offers mercy to you and to all those who are within your walls."

"How noble of him." Sir Godfrey snorted. "I find it strange that he comes with an army to offer mercy. What are his terms?"

"You must surrender this castle by nightfall.

If you do this and throw yourself on his mercy then all will be spared."

"*Never!*" Sir Godfrey roared. "This castle and these lands have belonged to our family since the time of King William. We will not surrender it. And we will not send these good people out to be butchered by your soldiers. John has never shown mercy before and he will not now. Begone!"

"Very well Sir Godfrey," said the man with a smile. "May your death be as honourable as your words, for John desires you to know that if you do not surrender by nightfall you, your family and all who have taken refuge with you will be slaughtered like pigs."

"John has no claim to this castle save that he is a thieving, shrivelled up rogue who bullies the weak. Leave now, scoundrel or I will have you killed!"

The man below drew a sword and held it pointing up in front of his face. "On guard then, and adieu!" The rider wheeled his horse around and galloped away, waving his sword over his head. As he did so, a slow, heavy drumbeat started up somewhere in the enemy ranks. It was picked up along the line until it thundered across the fields towards the castle from all directions.

"It's beginning," said Adam and he turned away.

"Archers, to the walls!" cried the sergeant over the din of the drums and for a while there was frenzied activity as men rushed up to join those already on the wall. Finn and Arthur stayed where they were, already in position while others ran to positions on the ground inside the wall and stood nervously next to supplies of water and piles of blankets. Fires were lit in stone-ringed pits by others. Thomas rushed past the boys with a breathless, "Good luck!"

Sir William emerged from the castle and mounted the steps to the outer wall. He walked along it, clapping each archer on the back and offering words of encouragement. When he got to Finn and Arthur he greeted them warmly.

"It is not our custom to send boys into battle but young Thomas informs me that you fought bravely earlier today. We will need all the bravery in all of our hearts before this night is over. Fight well boys." And he moved on. Everyone seemed to feel bigger and stronger after a few words from Sir William, and the boys were no exceptions.

Abruptly the drumbeat stopped. The shouting

inside the castle subsided and a tense hush fell over the whole scene. Somewhere a river bird screeched, getting on with its own business as the army of John the Withered waited for the signal to attack.

Finn stared over at Arthur, eyes round, nostrils flared, every sinew in his body taut like the bowstring in his fingers.

And then, through the still evening air came a creak and a whir as the arm of one enemy trebuchet swung up and over. Something shot up from the catapult, and sailed high through the air across the divide between attackers and defenders. Finn noted with a sick feeling in his stomach that whatever it was appeared to have arms and legs. It flew over the archers' heads and landed with a *whumpf* on the ground inside the wall. It was plain for all to see that the first missile from the attacking army had been a horribly misshapen corpse.

"Dogs!" bellowed Sir William. "You will pay!"

The enemy reply was a blast on a horn, followed by a whole chorus of creaks and whirs as each of the trebuchets released its load.

Round, black, smoking projectiles flew at the castle like burning crows. One landed on the parapet between Arthur and Finn with a splintering crash, and suddenly the wall between them was engulfed in fire.

"Tar pots!" shouted Finn. "They won't damage the wall but don't get the stuff on you!"

Arthur had no intention of getting anywhere near it. On the ground inside the wall, pools of fire were dotted around wherever the pots had landed. One poor soul was running around in bigger and bigger circles, wrapped from head to toe in flickering fire. Eventually someone managed to wrestle him to the ground with a blanket and extinguished the fire.

Someone brushed past Finn with another blanket and started to smother the fire on the wall. More tar pots flew in a regular, grinding bombardment and more fire splattered around the castle. The fire-fighters were at full stretch.

"They are advancing!" someone shouted urgently.

As fire rained down from the sky amid shouts of fear, the attacking soldiers marched forwards and the booming drumbeat resumed.

"*Archers make ready,*" called the Sergeant in

charge of the archery line. Finn and Arthur followed the lead of those to either side of them. They drew arrows back and angled their shots slightly upwards.

"*Release!*" boomed the Sergeant and a swarm of arrows arched towards the attackers, raining down on helmets and raised shields, heads and shoulders. Some men dropped to the ground but their comrades did not falter and stepped across the bodies, marching inexorably on.

"*Cover!*" called the Sergeant and the defenders all crouched down as a shower of enemy arrows hissed and fizzed over the battlements. A man to Arthur's left screamed in pain and toppled backwards off the wall spouting blood from an arrow wound to the neck.

"*Archers, ready,*" called the Sergeant again and a second volley of arrows flew at the attackers. More men fell and more bodies were trodden underfoot as the army continued its advance, running forward now getting closer and closer to the moat.

"*Shoot at will,*" roared the Sergeant and all semblance of order was lost. Under a hail of fire and arrows, Finn, Arthur and the other archers peered out from behind the cover of the battlements, lined up targets and shot them down.

Within seconds the advancing soldiers had reached the edge of the moat as behind them the attacking army's archers redoubled their assault until the castle defenders felt as though they were under a permanent dark cloud of arrows.

A second wave of soldiers arrived at the edge of the moat, carrying a makeshift wooden bridge that they hoisted up and allowed to topple forward across the water. As the attackers swarmed over the moat, most of the archers, previously spread around the whole of the outer wall, rushed over to join Finn and Arthur near the gatehouse. Boiling water was brought up the steps and distributed along this part of the wall and while the archers continued unleashing their deadly arrows down onto the heads of the attackers, the boiling water was hoisted up onto the battlements and poured down to burn any who tried to place ladders against the outer wall.

Finn was shaking with fear by this time. His arms were aching and his fingers were so slippery with sweat that he could barely grip his bowstring. Out of nowhere a ladder appeared on the other side of the wall in front of his face and he screamed for help. A man ran to his side with a long wooden pole and began to push the ladder away from the wall just as the first enemy head appeared at the battlements. Frantically Finn dropped his bow and grabbed the pole helping the man to heave the ladder away from the wall.

Slowly the ladder toppled backwards, sending the men on it crashing to the ground or into the moat. Finn looked across to find Arthur but then something stung his arm and he stumbled backwards in surprise. He lost his footing and with a cry for help he tumbled off the wall, his helmet knocked off his head as he fell. He landed on something soft, hit his head on something hard and lost consciousness.

EXTRACT FROM *WARRIOR HEROES*
BY FINN BLADE

CASTLE SIEGES

The whole point about a knights's
castle is that an enemy can never
get inside. They are made of rock,
built on top of steep mounds,
surrounded by moats and outer
walls, and full of nasty little
surprises like the holes through
which defenders can pour boiling
oil on their attackers. But if you
like a challenge, here are some of
the things people have come up with
to help break down castle defences:

BATTERING RAMS

These are huge tree trunks
tipped with iron which are hung

horizontally from wooden frames.
Teams of soldiers swing the trunk
back and then crash it forward
against the castle door to break it.

MISSILES

A range of huge catapults have
been designed to fire missiles
at or over castle walls from
a distance. The best of these
catapults can throw a heavy rock
very accurately over 200 metres.
But some people don't just use the
catapults to throw rocks…

• You can shoot firepots onto the
  castle roof to start fires.

• Or you could shoot dead animal
  corpses over the walls to spread
  disease.

• And if you really want to get

noticed, shoot the heads of dead
enemy soldiers over the walls to
terrify the poor souls inside
the castle!

UNDERMINING

Undermining means digging huge
warrens of tunnels underneath the
castle. The tunnels are propped
up with wooden struts and then
the wood is set on fire. When the
struts burn away, the tunnels, and
sometimes the castle walls, will
collapse.

SIEGE TOWERS

If you can't get under the walls
or smash your way through them then
there is only one other approach -
over the top. To do this you'll need

to build a wooden tower on wheels,
roll it up to the castle walls and
jump across.

SIT IT OUT

If all that sounds like too
much work there is an easier way.
Surround the castle with your army
and don't let any food or supplies
in. Then just sit back and wait.
Sooner or later the people inside
are going to want some lunch and
come out...

CHAPTER 5

The first thing Finn became aware of when he came to was the throbbing pain in his arm. He opened his eyes and tried to sit up, but as the room began to swim he quickly slumped back onto the straw he had been lying on.

"Steady there Finn," said Thomas, laying a hand on Finn's chest.

Finn looked, blurry-eyed, over to where

both Thomas and Arthur were sitting. Beside Thomas was the most beautiful girl Finn had ever seen. Her piercing blue eyes stared intently out from a fine-boned face, framed by long, black hair.

"Your wound is not serious but you do need to rest," she said kindly.

"And you need to get back to the keep my lady," said Thomas sternly.

"I will not spend any longer locked away in a big stone prison," she snapped. "The wounded need help. Everyone in here is risking their life to defend the castle and I do not wish to be any different."

"This is Eleanor," said Arthur. "In case you hadn't guessed."

"Wh... What happened to me?" Finn asked,

attempting to sit up once more and then instantly falling back down. "And what about the siege?"

Thomas explained that Finn had been struck in the arm by an arrow and fallen from the outer wall. He'd landed on a straw bale which luckily had broken his fall but he had hit his head on a cart wheel which had knocked him out. His arm had been bandaged by Eleanor who had been tending to the sick with her maids-in-waiting.

"You nearly made it to the end of the battle," said Arthur. "A few minutes after you fell the attack was over. You've been out cold all night."

"It's not the end though. John's army will come again soon enough," said Thomas grimly.

Finn looked around him for the first time.

He was lying in a small makeshift tent which appeared to be set up close to the outer wall. Through the open side of the tent he could see the effects of last night's carnage. The earth was scorched where the tar pots had done their damage and out from the bottom of a lumpy mound that was covered in matting, there protruded several legs and arms.

Following Finn's gaze Eleanor said quietly, "Too many people died last night. And all because of the greed of John the Withered. That is why we must fight him to the end."

"*You* need not fight him my lady," Thomas protested.

"Oh, forgive my mistake Thomas. Perhaps you would prefer it if I did what was expected of me and married a knight?"

Thomas looked crestfallen. "I do not mean to tell you what you can and cannot do. I just do not want you to be killed," he said, eyes averted.

Eleanor softened and gently said, "Perhaps you could accompany me as I visit the other wounded men."

Thomas perked up instantly and stood. "I will my lady," he said, puffing out his chest slightly. He nodded to Finn and Arthur. "Farewell for now friends."

"He's got it bad," Arthur chuckled as Thomas and Eleanor made to leave. But before they could, their paths were blocked by Sir Ralph at the entrance to the tent.

"My lady," panted Sir Ralph, "I have been looking everywhere for you. You really should not be out here with these..." he looked scornfully over at the boys. "It is too dangerous and this is no place for a young lady. Come back to the keep, you will be safe there." And he moved forward to take her by the arm.

"I will do no such thing," replied Eleanor, her eyes flashing dangerously as she stepped out of his reach. But Ralph ignored the signs.

"My lady, you know of my affections." He glanced at Thomas and smiled cruelly. "But I must insist now. Do as I say and get back to the keep. He held out an arm for Eleanor to take but she swiped it away."

"Men are all fools, Sir Ralph, but you are more foolish than most. I am not your child to order around. Nor are these others," she went on, indicating the boys.

Sir Ralph's face began its familiar transition to crimson. "You dare to..."

"Enough!" someone barked behind Sir Ralph. "Stand aside!" shouted Sir William as he strode into the tent.

"Sir William," Ralph spluttered. "I did not mean to – "

"I heard enough of what was said. My daughter is right, she is not yours to command. Now leave."

Fuming, Sir Ralph turned on his heel and stomped away.

"Father," Eleanor began.

"And Sir Ralph is right in part also – it is not safe for you to be out here. They will attack again at any moment. You must return to the keep. Immediately."

"But I want to help!" Eleanor implored.

"Then help by protecting yourself," her father replied curtly. "If I am worrying about you then I am not defending this castle as well as I might. This is not the time for us to argue Eleanor, please, go back."

With a face like thunder, Eleanor did as her father had asked. Sir William turned to Thomas. "Word reaches me that you fought bravely last night. You have my thanks. We will need that strength again today." He paused for a few moments. "Eleanor is very capable of a brave fight also, is she not?"

Thomas nodded, open-mouthed.

"She will find that there are some battles in life she cannot win. Marriage, for example," Sir William went on gently. "I wish it were not so, but she will not choose the man she marries, he will be chosen for her soon enough, and he will be a knight."

Thomas closed his mouth quickly and averted his gaze to the ground, his shoulders sagging slightly.

"These boys," said Sir William, turning to look at Arthur and Finn. "They are your friends?"

"Yes Sir."

"Then you seem to choose your friends wisely lad. Word has reached me that they too fought bravely last night. We must keep our spirits up Thomas or we will not prevail. You fought well and when this is over I will honour you all."

"Now," he said, turning away. "I must find Sir Godfrey. Perhaps you will come with me Thomas."

As they left the tent Finn groaned and rolled

over on his straw bed, clutching at his bandaged arm. Arthur frowned as he watched his brother grimace in pain.

"Finn, seriously, are you OK?"

"Yeah, apart from the fact I've been shot in the arm, almost died defending a castle against attack, and fell three metres only to get knocked out, I'm just great!"

"Well, we're both still here," said Arthur, trying to sound positive. "That's the main thing... right?"

"Yes but what are we going to do?" Finn groaned. "We need a plan to get Eleanor out. If Sir William was right about the spy then whoever it is must be in here with us somewhere. How are we going to persuade Eleanor to leave with us? And then how are we going to get out?"

"Beats me," Arthur shook his head. "I think all

we can do at the moment is try and survive – "

Both boys fell quiet, thinking about all they had seen the previous night.

"That was worse than anything we've – " Finn was interrupted by the Sergeant's booming voice. "Archers, to the walls. They come again!"

"I'd better go," said Arthur wearily. "If you feel better you could try and get inside the keep and see what you can find out. You were wounded in battle, surely they must trust you now."

"OK," said Finn. "And Arthur... be careful up there."

Arthur smiled nervously and walked out of the tent, putting on his helmet as he went.

Finn listened to the sounds of imminent battle, his head swimming with a panic of thoughts that went round and round in circles. *Get her out before the spy takes her. Try and stop the spy. How do we convince her to leave? How do we escape?* He felt dizzy. Nothing was clear. He let go of his thoughts and lay back, putting a hand over his eyes. Gradually, beneath the shouts of the soldiers up on the walls, Finn latched onto a different sound – the sound of a whispered conversation that seeped through the canvas of the tent.

"She walks freely around the castle and outside. Why wait until she is in the keep?"

"We cannot get her across the walls during the day. We have to do this at night."

Finn caught his breath. *The spy!* He could not believe his luck. Carefully, he rolled off the straw, trying not to lean on his injured arm and crawled to the side of the tent so that he could hear more clearly.

"And we must do it this very night. With every day that passes Sir William will be more and more concerned for her safety."

"Agreed. You have the potion?"

"Of course I do."

"Good. Then we must give it to her this night and she will sleep like the dead."

"But we have no way of entering her room."

"We will find a way. When the battle is raging we will not be heard."

The whispering stopped. Finn had to find out who they were without being seen. Putting his head to the ground, he lifted the side of the tent very carefully by just a few centimetres.

Rushing away from the tent was the unmistakable figure of Adam.

CHAPTER 6

Finn stumbled out of the tent and looked around him. Adam had disappeared and there was no sign of whoever he had been whispering with. An arrow hissed into the ground next to Finn making him jump and he quickly set off for the keep at a sprint.

He reached the doors and began hammering on them as hard as he could. There was no answer. All around him he could hear the crunches, crashes and cries of battle. *Of course they won't hear me*, he thought. *What do I do?* He looked back at the outer wall and saw Thomas running along it, carrying a burning torch and heading for a cluster of men a short distance from the gatehouse.

Finn's only thought now was to reach someone who would listen to him about the danger Eleanor was in. He sprinted over to the steps of the outer wall and bounded up them, the pain in his arm forgotten as a familiar mixture of fright and adrenalin numbed his nerves.

But as he reached the battlements he saw why the cluster of men had come together. Barely a metre away from the wall was the wooden tower that he and Arthur had seen the soldiers constructing the previous afternoon. The top of the tower was a little higher than the outer wall and several men were crammed inside it, all protected by a thick wall of wood. Some burning arrows were lodged in the timbers but so far none of the fire had taken hold.

Finn stood transfixed as all hell broke loose. A section of the tower clattered down like a drawbridge to make a platform linking the tower to the battlements. A group of soldiers thundered across it wielding swords, battleaxes and maces, swinging left and right at the defenders and forming a line of defence that protected their siege engine. The fighting had become even more savage than on the previous day and countless men toppled off either side of the wall.

Unarmed, Finn could do nothing but watch as the battle raged before him. More men had appeared on the platform of the siege engine and were preparing to leap over the battlements to join their comrades. But before they could, Finn saw Thomas lean out from the battlements and lob something at the platform. A shout went up from the attackers as the platform went up in flames and they were beaten back. One by one the first wave of soldiers to cross the wall were picked off until none of the enemy remained inside the wall. Tar pots were being handed round and were flung at the tower, the insides of which were now exposed by the lowered platform. Very soon the whole tower had become a roaring inferno.

Finn hunched down behind the battlements and made his way towards Thomas, who was being congratulated by a weary-looking Sir Godfrey. But before Finn had time to speak the Sergeant roared *"Battering ram! Archers ready! All other men to the castle gates!"* In seconds the wall to either side of the gatehouse was lined with archers while a crowd of others, including Thomas, sped down the steps and put their backs to the gates.

The great oak trunk, that the boys had seen the previous day had been sharpened to a point and tipped with iron. It swung back and forth, booming as the attackers smashed away at the castle gates, which shook and wobbled and creaked alarmingly. The archers above kept up a relentless shower of arrows but the men at the battering ram were well protected by a wooden roof that had been erected on top of the ram.

The gates began to make splintering noises and the Sergeant rushed down the steps, grabbing certain archers and telling them to follow.

"*Tar pots!*" He bellowed. "*Burning arrows!*"

Moments later he had three lines of men facing the gates.

"*Open!*" he cried and instantly the gates were unbolted and flung open.

"*Shoot!*" The first line of men released a volley of arrows into the faces of the nearest attackers.

"*Pots!*" The second line flung the tar pots straight at the battering ram and under its roof.

"*Shoot!*" The final line of men shot burning arrows out through the open gates.

"*Close!*" With the enemy in disarray, the

gates were slammed closed again. The archers who remained on the wall picked off soldiers on the ground who were darting out from under the now burning roof of the battering ram.

A horn blasted in the distance and a great shout went up among the defenders as the attacking army began to retreat again, back across the moat.

Finn caught sight of Arthur amongst the massed defenders and rushed to his side.

"Another attack foiled!" cried Arthur gleefully. "But what are you doing up here? Are you OK?"

"It's Eleanor!" Finn gasped, and he poured out the whole story. It was only as he finished that he noticed Adam standing behind Arthur, a murderous look on his face.

"Sir Ralph!" shouted Adam. "You must hear this, it concerns Eleanor."

"What?" Finn spluttered. "Wait!"

"Silence boy," said Sir Ralph, appearing behind Finn. "What did you wish to say Adam?"

Arthur tried to interrupt. "He's going to kid – "

"I said *silence*!" Ralph thundered, striking Arthur savagely across the face with the back of his hand and knocking Arthur's helmet off as he did so.

Arthur stumbled backwards, clutching his stinging face and the victorious cheering of the men died down as they noticed what was happening.

"I believe these boys are spies, Sir Ralph," said Adam calmly. "And I believe they plan to kidnap Lady Eleanor." Outrage and glee jostled for position on Sir Ralph's face.

"Can you prove it?" he asked.

"I think so. But we should get them down from the wall in case they try to escape."

"Quite right," said Sir Ralph. "You men, take these boys down to the ground and keep a good grip on them." But before any of the men could respond Adam stepped forward and grabbed Arthur, pushing him down the steps and following directly behind him. Sir Ralph followed quickly.

Thomas came running up to them. "What is happening?" he cried.

"We are about to find out whether your friends here have been entirely honest with us," Sir Ralph replied. "Adam, if you would like to fill this *young* squire in."

"You don't understand," wailed Finn. "It's Adam. He's going to – "

"*Let him speak!*" Ralph shouted.

"I thank you sir," said Adam. "I overheard the boys discussing a plot to kidnap Lady Eleanor and take her to John the Withered as a hostage. They mentioned a sleeping potion that would prevent the Lady from resisting."

"Search them," Ralph barked and two men stepped forward quickly to run their hands through the boys' clothes.

"This is madness!" said Thomas, but the words were barely out of his mouth when his eyes widened in shock. The man searching Arthur pulled out a small stone bottle from the boy's clothes.

"What?" Arthur exclaimed, pointing at Adam.

"He must have put it there when he brought me down the steps."

Sir William strode up to the group. "What is the meaning of all this?"

"This good man," said Sir Ralph, nodding to Adam, "informed me that he overheard these boys plotting to kidnap Eleanor as a hostage.

It is my belief that they are spies for John the Withered."

"Spies?" Sir William snorted. "But they are just boys – mere children. Friends of yours Thomas, isn't that right?"

Thomas said nothing, but stared from Finn to Arthur and back again.

"Thomas?"

"I believed that they were friends," he said coolly. "Finn saved my life. But in truth I met them only yesterday."

"Thomas!" cried Finn "You must know – "

"Be quiet!" snapped Sir William. "I can take no chances over a threat to my daughter. You will be imprisoned in the keep until I have time to investigate the matter further. Take them away."

"But you have to believe the threat is Adam.

Watch him!" Finn shouted as he and Arthur were hauled away, both struggling against the iron grips of their guards.

They had wanted to see the inside of the keep, but as they entered it for the first time, they immediately longed to be outside again. They were led through dark halls, gloomy passages, and down a narrow staircase into a damp, cold basement. A couple of torches gave off just enough light to see by, and as the boys were pushed into a small, windowless room, the door slammed behind them and they were both struck by the grim realisation that they were now locked in a medieval dungeon.

EXTRACT FROM *WARRIOR HEROES*
BY FINN BLADE

MEDIEVAL WEAPONS
ARMOUR

If you are a knight with a bit
of cash you'll wear chain mail, or
heavy metal plates as armour, or
both. This is good for stopping
arrows and blades. Not so good for
getting around quickly, or getting
out of a moat if you fall in. On the
other hand if you're an ordinary
soldier you'll probably just wear
some heavy leather clothes to try
and keep the swords at bay.

Of course you'll use the usual
warrior's kit - sword, axe, knife,
bow and arrow, spear and shield.
You could also choose to use one of
these interesting options…

MACE

A mace is essentially something very heavy on the end of a handle. The heavy part could be made of metal or stone, and the handle from wood or sometimes metal. It's like a sledge hammer which is quite good if you're attacking someone with heavy armour as you don't have to get through the armour to hurt them. You just bash them over the head.

FLAIL

A particularly effective variation on the mace is the flail, which is a heavy metal ball with spikes all over it, attached to a stick by a length of chain. You can do some serious damage with this weapon.

HALBERD

Think of a spear (for stabbing not throwing). Then add an axe blade on one side of the shaft near the spear point. And then add a nasty metal hook on the other side of the shaft. You can use this to stab like a spear, swing like an axe, or pull someone off balance (or off their horse) without getting too close.

CHAPTER 7

Time seemed to change its meaning that day. Locked underground with no natural light and left to stew on their fears of what might follow, the boys began to lose hope.

"They wouldn't torture a pair of kids..." said Arthur. "Would they?"

Finn nodded his head slowly, sick with dread. "Sir William thinks we're spies and this siege could go on for months. He'll do anything to defend the castle. I don't think they had child protection laws in Medieval England."

Strange grunts, scrapes and oaths echoed down the stone corridor and both boys shifted uncomfortably on the hard, cold floor.

Finn remembered the Professor talking about castles and dungeons. He knew that in medieval times most castles didn't have real prisons or dungeons as such. Imprisonment wasn't a common punishment – execution was far more likely.

"Although if they really want to torment someone they might use an oubliette." Finn said thoughtfully.

"Eh?" said Arthur.

"Nothing," said Finn quickly. He hadn't

intended to mention the oubliette out loud. It didn't exist in all castles but it was used for the most horrible-sounding punishment he had heard of. An oubliette was a deep shaft in the ground with a lid on the top. The shaft was often so narrow that there was only room to stand and breathe. You couldn't sit, lie down or even turn around. It was literally a manhole. If they really wanted someone to suffer they would lower the poor wretch into the oubliette, stick the lid on, leave them in total darkness and forget about them. In fact the word oubliette came from the French "to forget." Finn shivered at the thought of it.

"Come on." Arthur urged. "There must be some way out of this."

"We're locked in a dungeon underneath a

castle, Arthur. I don't think there is a way out this time."

"Well think of something," snapped Arthur. "You always think of something."

"Really? What do you think our chances are?" Finn asked sarcastically. "We'll have to find Eleanor and convince her that she has to come with us even though her dad thinks we're here to kidnap her, then we'll have to find a way out of the castle in the middle of a siege, and if by some miracle we manage all of that we'll have to get past an army that has the castle completely surrounded. So no Arthur, I don't think I'm going to think of *something* this time!"

Finn stared miserably through a grate in the door. A shadowy wall of damp stone stared back at him in the faint torchlight.

"Not that it matters," he sighed. "We won't even get as far as that wall."

"Finn!" Arthur shouted, getting to his feet. "Get a grip. If we can't break out then we'll have to think our way – "

His words dried up in his throat as the sound of boots approaching rang along the passage and in seconds Sir Ralph had appeared at the grill in the door and peered in at them with a sneer. Neither of the boys could meet his stare.

"I came to see how the boy spies are liking their new home," he mocked. "I told you I would make you pay," he went on, glancing at Arthur. "But I must confess I did not see things shaping up this nicely. You may remember that Sir William's punishment for spies is death, yes?" Finn winced at this but Arthur looked up.

"You know it wasn't us!" he shouted, fists clenched in fury. "You were there! Why was Adam so keen to be the one who pushed me down the steps? He planted that bottle on me."

"Really?" Sir Ralph replied lazily. "Perhaps. Still, nobody else saw anything wrong did they?"

"How can you be so stupid?" Finn chimed in, scrambling to his feet to stand beside his brother. "Can't you see that if Adam is the spy then Sir William is not safe and neither is Eleanor. The castle will fall and you could have prevented it."

"Really?" Sir Ralph repeated in the same casual way.

Suddenly Finn saw what was happening and the thought made him feel sick. Ralph did know that Adam was the spy and he didn't care.

He wanted Adam to carry on. He wanted the castle to fall.

"You... you *do* know don't you?"

"The castle will fall, you are right," replied Ralph, ignoring Finn's comment. "But Eleanor will be quite safe, I will see to that."

"How can you think that she will even look at you when she finds out what you're doing?" Arthur spat.

"Ha!" Sir Ralph exclaimed. "The girl really won't have much choice in the matter by the time John the Withered has finished here."

The boys were too shocked to speak.

"You do look wretched in there you know," he went on. "But here is something that will cheer you up. In a few minutes you will have some company." He emitted a cruel laugh that set the boys' teeth on edge. What could he mean?

"Well, I must tell you that I have enjoyed our little discussion. I don't think we'll be seeing each other again." With that Sir Ralph's face disappeared from the grill.

Finn and Arthur sat in silence. There was nothing to say. Adam would kidnap Eleanor. Sir Ralph would weaken the defences somehow. John the Withered would sack the castle and Sir William and all the rest would probably be killed. For their own part the boys knew that they would probably die even sooner at the hands of Sir William who had been fooled by Adam and Sir Ralph's trickery and this, of course, was the most dismal thought of all.

"I wonder what the Professor would have

done..." mused Finn, but neither boy could think of an answer.

Some time later a clatter of boots reached the boys' ears. Sick with dread as they awaited their fate, they shrank to the back of the cell. The footsteps stopped outside their cell and the door was unlocked and wrenched open.

"In there," a gruff voice barked, as someone was shoved through the door and sent sprawling to the floor.

"Thomas!" cried Finn as he recognised his friend. "What's happening? We thought you were the executioner."

"I may as well have been," Thomas replied, getting back to his feet. "I cannot apologise enough that I did not believe you earlier. Adam and Sir Ralph are plotting together."

"We know," said Arthur. "He came and told us all about it the smug fool. But how did you end up down here?"

"I heard them plotting to attack Sir William during battle and make it look like an accident. When they saw that I had overheard them they did the same to me as they had to you, only this time they planted a letter in my pocket – a letter from one of John's knights.

"I could see that Sir William had his doubts but he can take no risks now. So here we are, back together again. Tell me, what did Ralph say to you?"

Arthur filled Thomas in, not noticing Finn's attempts to steer him off the subject of Eleanor until it was too late. By the time Arthur had finished Thomas was in a state of complete desolation. Finn wished he could say something comforting, but it seemed there really was nothing to say and the three prisoners sank into a brooding silence again, each lost in his own dark and desperate thoughts.

CHAPTER 8

Hours had passed before Finn's unhappy reverie was broken by the sight of dark shadows leaping on the damp stone walls outside their cell.

"Arthur. Thomas," Finn whispered, frowning through the darkness. "Someone's coming."

Once again they retreated to the back of the cell as a hooded figure appeared at the door and all three boys held their breath, not daring to move. Whoever it was looked each way along the passage, and then a key turned gently in the lock, allowing the door to swing open. Finn thought he saw a lock of long, black hair and a faint spark of hope rose in his chest. The hood was thrown back.

"Eleanor," the three of them gasped at once.

"Quiet!" she hissed.

Thomas rushed forward and embraced her, elated. It was only as she gently pushed him away that the boys could see her face clearly – tear-stained, pale and drawn it was a picture of grief.

"Eleanor, my love," Thomas soothed, "What has happened?"

"Father lies dying in his bed," she sobbed. "They say he was struck by an axe, fighting on the wall."

Thomas paled. "No. And what of Sir Godfrey and the castle?"

"Sir Godfrey lives and the castle has not yet fallen," said Eleanor, her voice cracking. "But it will fall soon. My father sent me here to..." she broke off, breath coming too fast and held a hand to her chest for a moment.

"...he wanted me to release you because he knows now that Sir Ralph is the traitor, not you, she went on. He wanted me to bring you to him. He would not say for what purpose but he said that we must not be seen. He does not know how many men's minds may have been poisoned by Ralph's treachery."

Arthur and Finn looked at one another knowingly.

"He sees what is coming," said Arthur quietly.

"We must go now," said Eleanor. "He has not long to live."

Thomas reached a comforting hand out to her but she shook her head and turned. "You need to follow me now."

Eleanor led them out of the dungeon and along the stone passage past similar rooms once full of food and other supplies but now almost empty. They climbed a flight of steps and as they emerged from the basement they heard the dreaded drumbeat that had announced the first attack on the castle, while over the sound of the drums came another booming sound they all recognised. The battering ram.

"Father says the defence will not hold much longer," said Eleanor, speeding up and dashing through an empty hall to a door set in a curved stone wall.

"This must be one of the towers," Finn whispered to Arthur as they began climbing an uncomfortably narrow spiral staircase. Through the occasional narrow slit in the stone they could see that it was dusk outside, and smoke and screams filled the air.

"Who goes there?" came a gruff voice and the boys froze.

"It is I and three friends," Eleanor replied. The boys could see nothing of what was happening due to the twisting of the stairs, but in a moment they heard a door opening and their party began to move again. They followed her past a guard who nodded to them and on towards two more guards blocking the next door who parted when they saw Eleanor approaching and opened the door for the group to enter a dimly lit bedroom.

Propped up on a pile of cushions lay Sir William, still in his chain mail and bleeding heavily through it. His eyes were glassy and his face a terrible shade of grey.

Eleanor ran to him and knelt at his side, sobbing.

"Did you find the boys, my child?" Sir William wheezed. "My eyes have failed me. Are they here?"

"We are here Sir William," said Thomas hoarsely.

"Ah, Thomas my boy. It was wrong of me to doubt you. My judgement was clouded with fear. Fear for the castle. Fear for Eleanor. Will you forgive a dying man?"

"There is nothing to forgive Sir William," he said quietly as tears filled his eyes.

"And your two friends. They fought so bravely for us and I branded them liars and spies. Boys, where are you?"

Finn and Arthur stepped forward, uncertain of what they should do.

"They are here, Father," said Eleanor gently.

"Good... Good. This battle is nearly over and John will have his way in a few more hours. Sir Ralph has been plotting against us from the first and now I lie dying..." Sir William coughed horribly, and a trickle of blood seeped from his lips. He lay silent.

"Father no!" cried Eleanor, stroking his head. With what seemed like a huge effort, Sir William spoke again.

"The castle will fall, that is certain. I will die, that is also certain and tragically so will most of those who fought alongside us. I have failed to protect them but there is one thing I can still protect... The most precious thing of all..." he squeezed Eleanor's hand. "You must live. You must escape."

"Father no. How can I live and let you die?"

"You *must* live Eleanor." Sir William insisted. "If I know that you will live then my death may not have been entirely worthless and if you do not escape then you will either die or be taken against your will by Ralph to live a life that feels like death. Make your escape child, you and Thomas and these boys."

"Father, no, please."

"Eleanor it is my dying wish, you may not

argue with me on this. Godfrey knows. He will stay and fight to hold John back for as long as possible. But he will not confront Ralph until you are gone. You must escape. Live, grow and one day you may find a way to reclaim this castle for your family. That is my wish child." Again he broke off and coughed more blood onto his chin.

"Thomas, my boy. You will protect my daughter."

"With my life, Sir William."

"Then there is one last act I must perform," said the knight, speaking in barely more than a croak now. "Somebody pass me my sword."

Arthur had seen Sir William's sword at his bedside the moment they entered the room and now he reached for it. He laid the sword on the

bed next to Sir William and placed the dying man's hand on the hilt.

"Thomas I said to you yesterday that my daughter would one day soon marry a knight. So kneel."

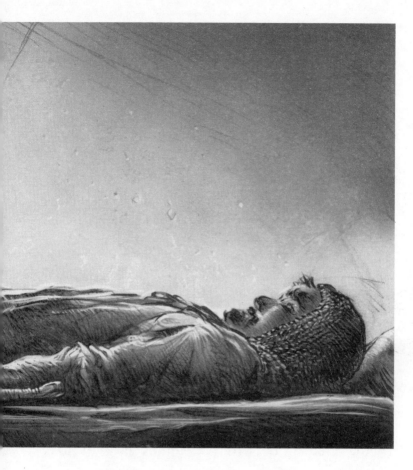

Open-mouthed, Thomas fell to his knees beside Sir William.

"Place your hands on mine, Thomas, on this sword."

Thomas did as he was told.

"If you wish to marry my daughter then you have my blessing. Protect her as I have done. No, protect her better than I have done. Take her from here, and take your two friends also, they are too young to die in battle. Take this sword of mine and make good your escape. Now, arise Sir Thomas Shipton."

Thomas stood, tears streaming down his cheeks. Eleanor lay her head on her father's chest and sobbed.

"Boys," Sir William whispered. "There are more weapons in the chest beside the bed. Take them." Gently, he lifted Eleanor's face in his hands and smiled.

"Now go," he whispered. "Before it is too late."

Unable to speak, Eleanor kissed his forehead

and stood. Thomas placed an arm around her shoulders as Finn and Arthur each took an armful of weapons and followed them to the door.

"Goodbye Father," Eleanor sobbed, turning back.

"Goodbye my love," he replied. "Goodbye children. And good luck."

EXTRACT FROM *WARRIOR HEROES*
BY FINN BLADE

BECOMING A KNIGHT IN THREE SIMPLE STEPS

STEP 1: Try to make sure your dad
is a knight, then get the lord of
the local castle to take you on
as a page at around eight years
old. You'll be taught how to fight
with wooden spears and swords,
and how to ride a horse properly.
Unfortunately you'll also have
normal lessons in reading, writing,
Latin and possibly dancing and
essential fighting techniques. Get
really good at all this stuff.

STEP 2: When you're around sixteen
you should be made a squire. This
is supposed to be a promotion from

being a page and you will get to
learn how to fight properly - how
to joust, fighting in heavy armour,
using real weapons etc. But you'll
also have to be a servant to a
knight, serving him all his meals,
cleaning up after him, carrying
his things on the way to jousts and
possibly going with him to battle to
look after the tent while he's out
killing people.

STEP 3: When you're around twenty
you'll be knighted if people think
you're ready or if they really
need a few more knights for a
battle that's coming up. Your lord
will 'dub' you a knight. Forget
all this gentle tapping of swords
on shoulders. Originally part of
the dubbing ceremony involved the

squire getting punched and knocked over, presumably to remind them of what they were really there for.

Congratulations, you're now a knight! Now your lord can order you into battle whenever he feels like it.

CHAPTER 9

As the two guards outside the room closed the door behind them, Arthur turned to Eleanor.

"Eleanor can we speak in front of these guards?" She nodded, tears still streaming down her face and Arthur went on. "We are so very sorry about your father, and I hate to do this so quickly but we have to make a plan. How do we get out of the castle? We don't want Ralph to see us and we can't be spotted by the attackers either."

"Is there an escape tunnel?" Finn asked hopefully.

Eleanor shook her head and took a deep breath. "If Father wants us to escape and survive then we will need some rope. Can you both swim?" The boys nodded.

"Good," she went on. "Father always said that the only way to escape Wroxley Castle in a siege would be along the river, downstream from the mill. The keep drops straight down to the bank there and there is no outer wall."

Arthur shivered. He had nearly died in that river. It was weird to think that he only survived because Adam was there and wanted a friend to help get him into the castle.

"We'll need to get back to the cellars for rope," said Thomas.

"I will go alone," said Eleanor and before Thomas could protest she raised her hands, "I know, I know, you want to protect me but think – if I am seen nobody will question why I am there. However, if you are seen we will be attacked. I am safer – *we are all safer* – if I go alone. Wait here, I will be gone just a few minutes."

"At least take a sword," said Arthur, handing one over. She nodded, fastened the sword belt around her waist, touched Thomas' arm and exited the small corridor onto the staircase.

Thomas began pacing around immediately.

"I should go after her," he muttered after a few silent minutes had passed.

"No," Finn said. "She's right. We all have a better chance if we stay here."

Thomas turned to the guards. "You know what has happened?" They nodded.

"Nobody other than Sir Godfrey is to enter Sir William's room, and if you see Adam or Ralph..."

"We will kill them instantly," growled one of the guards.

"Thank you," said Thomas, and began pacing again.

"Where will we go from the river?" asked Finn at length, keen to keep Thomas talking.

"I do not know," he replied. "But if we can get past the enemy line it will be dark and Eleanor and I know the land well. We will have to be careful but all of John's men will be attacking Wroxley Castle so perhaps we might make our escape unnoticed. The hardest task will be getting into the river unseen, and swimming past the enemy."

"Who goes there?" barked the guard on the stairs, and then the door opened again and Eleanor reappeared carrying a length of rope and a few dark brown cloaks. Thomas rushed to her side.

"Put these on," she said, throwing the cloaks to the floor. "We will not be seen so easily." Moments later all four of them were cloaked, hooded and armed with an assortment of daggers, swords, bows and arrows.

Eleanor looked longingly at the door to her father's room and then turned away. "Follow me," she said.

She led them down the stairs a short way, then

along an unfamiliar passage and into an empty round room like a landing between two more twisting flights of stairs.

"This is the place," she said. "From here we can climb straight down to the river." Thomas uncoiled the rope and tied one end to a thick pillar in the middle of the room while Eleanor peered out through a small window.

"Good," she said. "Complete darkness and no moon."

Thomas took the loose end of the rope and fed it steadily out through the window until the small remaining section pulled at the pillar.

"I will go first in case of any surprises at the bottom," he said. "Eleanor, you follow, then Arthur. Finn, while each of us is climbing down watch over us with your bow at the ready."

Arthur put a hand on Thomas' shoulder. "Wait, what happens when we get to the bottom, or if we get separated?"

"At the bottom of the castle wall is a very thin ledge of earth before a steep bank. We should be able to wait there and then enter the river together. If we are separated then we should gather on the other side of the first bridge we come across. It is nearly half a mile away but the current is strong at the moment and it will not take long to reach."

"Can we find anything to float with?" Asked Finn nervously. "Perhaps we could try and break one of these doors up."

"There will be too much noise and it will take too long," said Eleanor. "We must go now."

Thomas nodded to the boys, kissed Eleanor's hand, and climbed awkwardly through the small window. Finn poked his bow through and leaned out after him, an arrow notched and ready to shoot at the first sign of any danger. Hand over hand on the rope, Thomas lowered himself to the bottom, walking his feet down the side of the castle wall.

The attack seemed to have intensified even more around the walls near the gatehouse, and while the fighting sounded more frantic than ever, around the corner by the river the wall appeared to be deserted.

"Your turn," said Finn, making way for

Eleanor to climb through the window. "See you at the bottom."

Again Finn acted as lookout and again there was no sign of any direct threat outside but as Eleanor reached the ground Finn and Arthur heard footsteps on the stairs inside the tower.

Finn ducked back inside and looked at Arthur, eyes wide in panic.

"Quick," Arthur hissed, "we'll go together. Out!"

Finn threw his bow over his head and scrambled out through the window, clutching at the rope as he lowered himself a few feet down the wall before steadying himself and gripping the rope tightly. He looked up to see that Arthur had followed quickly behind him.

"OK, go!" Arthur instructed as soon as he

was out, and the two boys slipped and snatched their way down as quickly as they could. They had not yet reached the ground when Finn heard a door opening, then a shout. He looked down and saw Thomas and Eleanor staring up from the ground, still nearly ten metres below.

"Go now!" he shouted down to them as a shout of alarm came from the window above.

"They've seen us!" yelled Arthur and Finn looked up again to see the outline of a head sticking out from the window.

"I'll kill you, you little rats!" Finn recognised Ralph's furious voice. The rope burned through his hands and he slid painfully down as fast as he dared.

"He'll cut the rope," Arthur shouted. "We have to jump!" Finn knew he was right. He kicked out

from the wall and let go of the rope, praying that he would clear the river bank and land in the water. Time slowed and the fall seemed to last an age. Then a wall of freezing water smacked Finn in the back and he gasped as the torrent took hold of his body and dragged him away.

He heard a splash and twisted around. At first he could see nothing but swirling water, but then Arthur's head bobbed up, coughing and cursing. Finn lay on his back and let the current take him. The cries and screams of battle grew louder as the river took him past the entrance to the moat that ran around to the gatehouse, though he could see nothing of the fighting. The shadowy outline of the castle began to recede and within a minute had been swallowed up by the night.

He drew breath, thinking he would call out

to find out whether Eleanor and Thomas were ahead of him but thought better of it as he remembered they may not yet be clear of the attacking army. Turning onto his front, he swam on with the freezing current until he began to make out the dark shape of a small stone bridge up ahead. He tried to kick closer to the bank but the river was too strong and his wounded arm, which he had barely noticed for the past day, now throbbed painfully as he passed under the arch of the bridge.

The rushing roar of the river intensified up ahead and Finn heard Eleanor's voice calling.

"Finn, stand up!"

He felt something scrape against his knee and thrust down with his feet to find he was sliding across shallow water over slippery pebbles and rocks. He stood up, staggering as the river tried to suck him forwards, and turned in time to see Arthur heading straight for him. Moments later the boys were holding hands as they slipped and wobbled their way to the river bank and finally slumped onto dry land, exhausted and freezing but alive, and reunited with Eleanor and Thomas.

CHAPTER 10

It was long past midnight by the time the wretched, shivering party dragged the door of a shepherd's hut closed behind them and sank to the floor.

"Fire," Thomas croaked through chattering teeth. Arthur found a small pile of dry wood and set to work building a fire in a pit at the centre of the hut. Eleanor found some sheepskins and everyone huddled close around the pit as the fire grew steadily hotter until steam from their wet clothes mixed with the wood-smoke and they gradually began to feel a little better.

They stared into the flames, each of them lost in thoughts about all they had been through, until Arthur wondered out loud, "What next?"

"What next?" Eleanor responded. "Well if we are going to live then we had better eat." She produced some cheese and salted pork from a bag she had carried under her cloak. "It is a little bit wet of course so if you would prefer to wait..." she broke off and handed the food around. "You all look hungry."

They tore into the food, devouring it in seconds, and for a while they forgot their sorrows. They were not out of danger but they had survived, and it felt good. Arthur made everyone laugh with an impression of Ralph at the window. Eleanor teased Thomas about being a great knight, and Finn teased both of them about getting married.

"Well, you must join us at the wedding," Eleanor laughed. "We could not have done this without your help." Finn looked sadly at Arthur.

"She is right," said Thomas. "You have both done so much. You have saved both of our lives and in merely two days have proved yourselves to be the truest of friends."

A sudden knock at the door silenced the room and for a moment nobody dared move. Eventually, Thomas slowly got to his feet, drew his sword and with a fleeting look to the rest of the group he hauled the door open. An old man stood in the doorway, his hands held out.

"We mean no harm," said the man.

"Are you with John the Withered?" Thomas demanded, pointing his sword directly at the man. "How many of you are there? Why are you here?"

"I am a shepherd and this is my hut," the man replied. "John's men burned our village to the ground and only a few survived. May we enter?" The man stepped aside to reveal a group of five men and women and two small children all looking frightened.

"I recognise this man Thomas," said Eleanor, getting to her feet. "He worked on my father's land. Let them in."

Seeing no threat, Thomas stood aside and ushered the group into the hut.

"You are kind my lady," said the old man. None of the new arrivals would look Eleanor in the eye.

"Just as my father was," Eleanor replied, eyes glassing over. "Wroxley Castle will fall soon. We cannot stay here long."

"I thought as much," said the old man. "Where will you go?"

"My father lives some fifty miles from here and he will give us all safe refuge," said Thomas. "It will be a dangerous journey but far less dangerous than staying here. John's men will put all their energy into the attack on the castle for a short while longer but then some of them will disband and I would not want to be discovered by those devils following on from sacking a castle.

"This hut may well have saved our lives,

old man," Thomas continued. "If you wish to accompany us to my father's house then we would be honoured."

"You too are kind, sir, and we will certainly come with you," said the man. "May I ask your name?"

"This," said Arthur proudly, "is Sir Thomas Shipton."

* * *

Finn woke with a start and sat up. His arm throbbed from the arrow wound, his head throbbed from the freezing river and his back ached from sleeping on a hard floor. Not quite knowing why but following instinct, he crept to the door and slipped out of the hut, surprised to find Arthur already there.

Away to the east the first rays of the morning

sun were lancing across the sky. They saw now that the hut they had slept in sat at the top of a long ridge and as they looked down into a valley they saw a sea of morning mist floating below them.

Arthur looked at Finn and smiled as the mist began to swirl and tumble up the side of the valley like an avalanche in reverse.

"Eleanor's safe now," said Finn.

"We're going home!" Arthur shouted as the mist enveloped them, growing thicker and thicker until they could not see one another and the hut, the valley, the castle and their friends vanished completely.

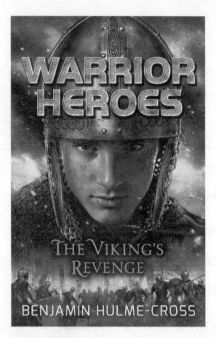

WARRIOR HEROES
The Viking's Revenge

Benjamin Hulme-Cross

Trapped in their great grandfather's museum by a
group of terrifying ghosts, Arthur and Finn must
travel back in time and help restore the famous
Viking sword, Blood Hunter, to its rightful owner
and escape the clutches of a fearsome Viking tribe.

£4.99

9781472904492

Extract from
WARRIOR HEROES
The Viking's Revenge

Arthur shivered, wondering where the cruel screeching was coming from. His cold bones ached. His face was wet and his nostrils were full of the smells of leaves and mud. He didn't want to wake up but as soon as you think that, you always do.

Find Blood Hunter!

He rolled over onto his back and opened his eyes, slowly letting in the thin dawn light. A spider crawled out of his hair and down his cheek. The birds kept screeching.

"Finn!" he croaked. Looking around he saw trees in all directions. *I must be in a forest somewhere,* he thought. He scanned the trees for any sign of his younger brother. Nothing.

Arthur had no idea where he was. He concentrated hard and an image of an old man looking down at him very seriously flashed before his eyes. His name danced around the edges of Arthur's memory. "Good luck," he said "and be brave." Then another man stepped into view, huge and bearded, wearing a helmet. Arthur's memories rushed into focus: Professor Blade; the Hall of Heroes; the Viking; *Find Blood Hunter!*